WHAT!
CRIED GRANNY
An *Almost* Bedtime Story

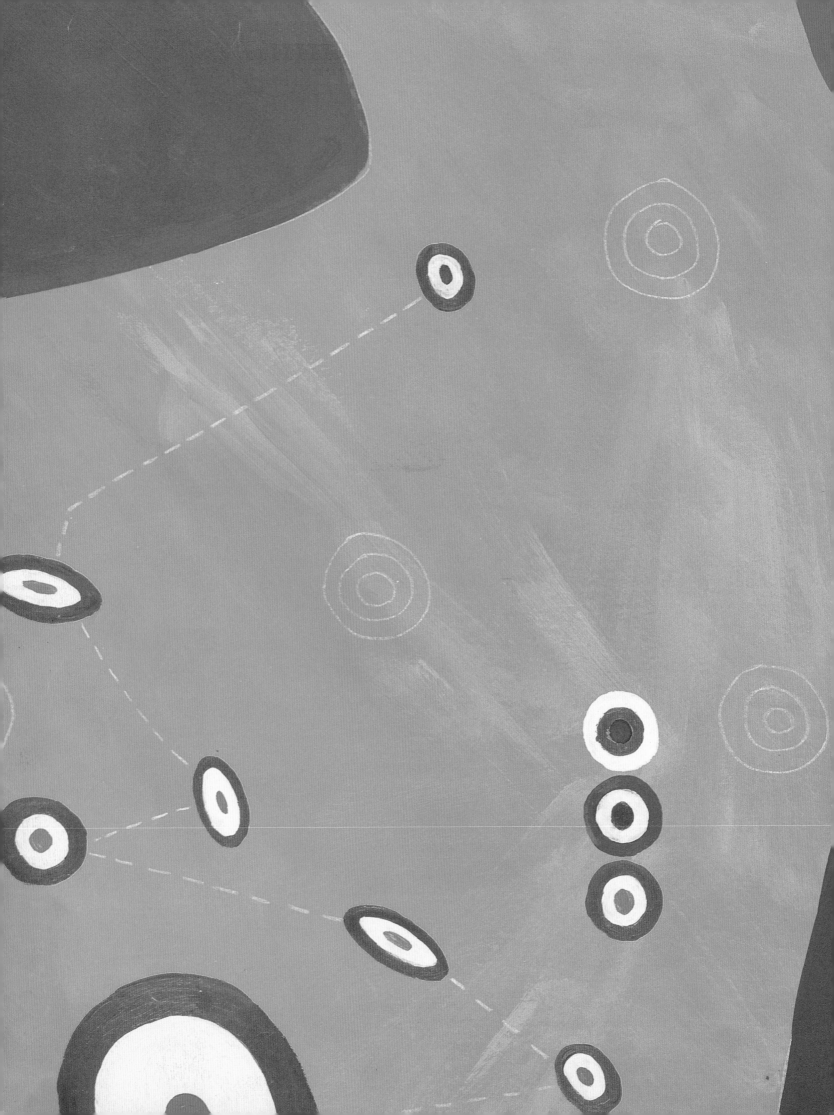

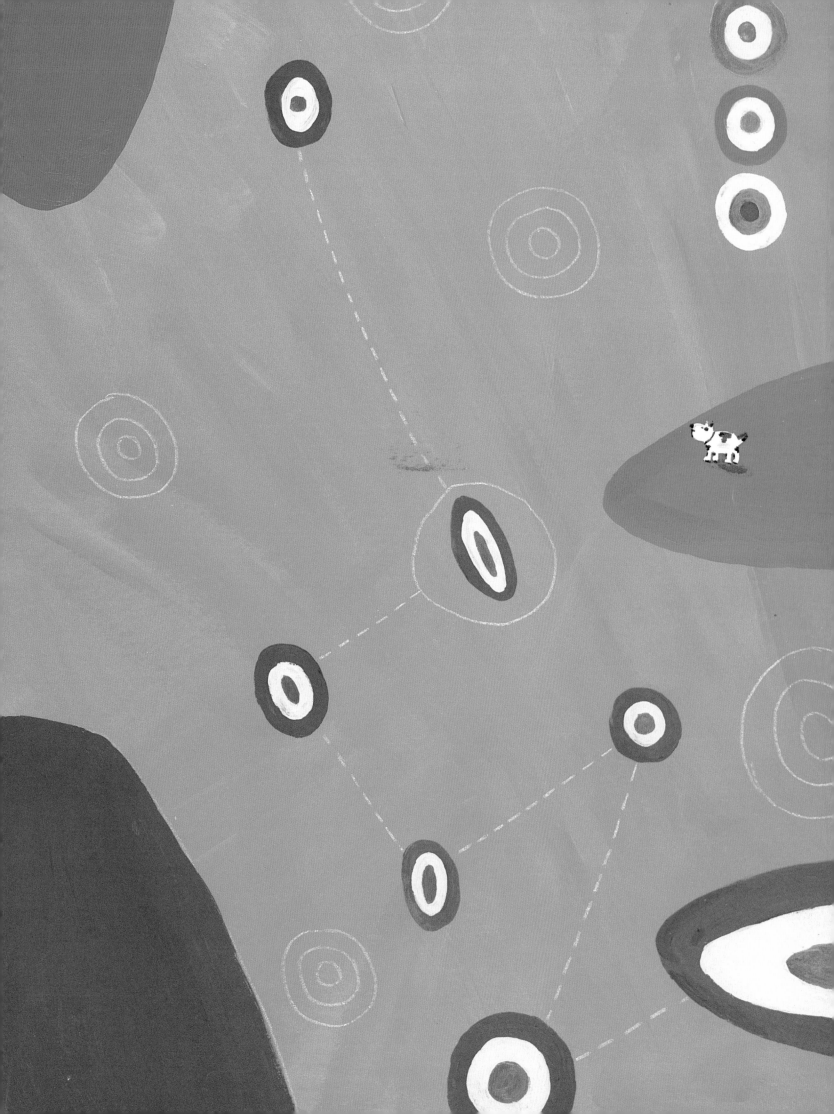

To the real Patrick, of course
K. L.

For Gran
A. J.

PUFFIN BOOKS
Published by the Penguin Group
Penguin Putnam Books for Young Readers,
345 Hudson Street, New York, New York 10014, U.S.A.
Penguin Books Ltd, 80 Strand, London WC2R ORL, England
Penguin Books Australia Ltd, Ringwood, Victoria, Australia
Penguin Books Canada Ltd, 10 Alcorn Avenue, Toronto, Ontario, Canada M4V 3B2
Penguin Books (N.Z.) Ltd, 182-190 Wairau Road, Auckland 10, New Zealand

Penguin Books Ltd, Registered Offices: Harmondsworth, Middlesex, England

Published in Great Britain by Bloomsbury Publishing Plc as *What!*, 1998
First published in the United States of America by Dial Books for Young Readers, a member of Penguin Putnam Inc., 1999
Published by Puffin Books, a division of Penguin Putnam Books for Young Readers, 2002

7 9 10 8

Text copyright © Kate Lum, 1998
Illustrations copyright © Adrian Johnson, 1998
All rights reserved

LIBRARY OF CONGRESS CATALOGING-IN-PUBLICATION DATA IS AVAILABLE UPON REQUEST

Puffin Books ISBN 0-14-230092-6

Manufactured in China

The artwork was prepared using acrylic paint on art board.

WHAT!
CRIED GRANNY
An *Almost* Bedtime Story

by **Kate Lum** pictures by **Adrian Johnson**

PUFFIN BOOKS

Once upon a time there was a boy named Patrick who was having his first sleep-over at his Granny's house.

As the sun began to set, Granny said, "Patrick, dear boy!
It will be dark soon. Time to get ready for bed."
"But, Granny," said Patrick....

"I don't **HAVE** a bed here."

"WHAT?"

cried Granny. She ran
out to her yard
where some tall
trees were growing, and
chopped one down.

She carried it to her workroom, opened her toolbox, and made Patrick a fine bed.

Then she painted it a restful shade of blue, put a comfy red mattress on it, and took it to the bedroom.

"There you are dear boy," said Granny. "Now climb
into bed, lay your head on the pillow, and sail
off to Dreamland!"

"But, Granny," said Patrick....

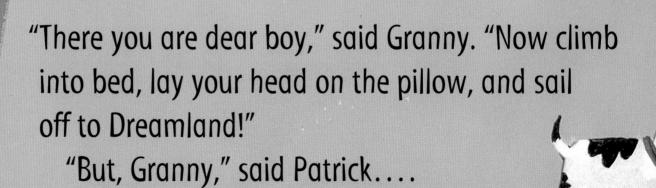

"I don't HAVE a pillow here!"

"WHAT?!?" cried Granny.
She ran out to her henhouse, woke up the chickens,
and collected a big batch of feathers.

She took them to her sewing room where she made
a bag out of cloth. Then she stuffed it with the feathers,
sewed it up neatly, and gave it to Patrick.

"There you are, dear boy," said Granny.
"Now climb into bed, lay your head on the pillow,
tuck the blanket under your chin, and I'll kiss you
good night."

"But, Granny," said Patrick....
"I don't **HAVE** a blanket here!"

"WHAAAT??!!??" cried Granny.
She ran outside and headed for the hills where
a flock of fat sheep were snoozing. She sheared
off some of their wool and ran right back home.

She took the wool to her basement, spun it into yarn, knitted a fuzzy warm blanket, and dyed it the prettiest shade of twilight purple. When it was dry, she carried it upstairs and spread it on the bed.

"Now, dear boy," said Granny, "climb into bed, lay your head on the pillow, tuck the blanket under your chin, give your teddy bear a hug, and turn out the light!"

"But, Granny," said Patrick....

"WHAAAAT?!!?" cried Granny.

She grabbed her emergency sewing kit, tore down the living room curtains, cut, sewed, stuffed, added button eyes and a red ribbon, and made a teddy bear for Patrick.

"NOW, PATRICK!" cried Granny.

"CLIMB into bed.

LAY your head on the pillow.

TUCK the blanket under your chin.

GIVE your teddy bear a hug.

And ...

GO TO SLEEP!"

"But, Granny," said Patrick....

"It's morning."

"WHAAAAAAA!!!!"

cried Granny.

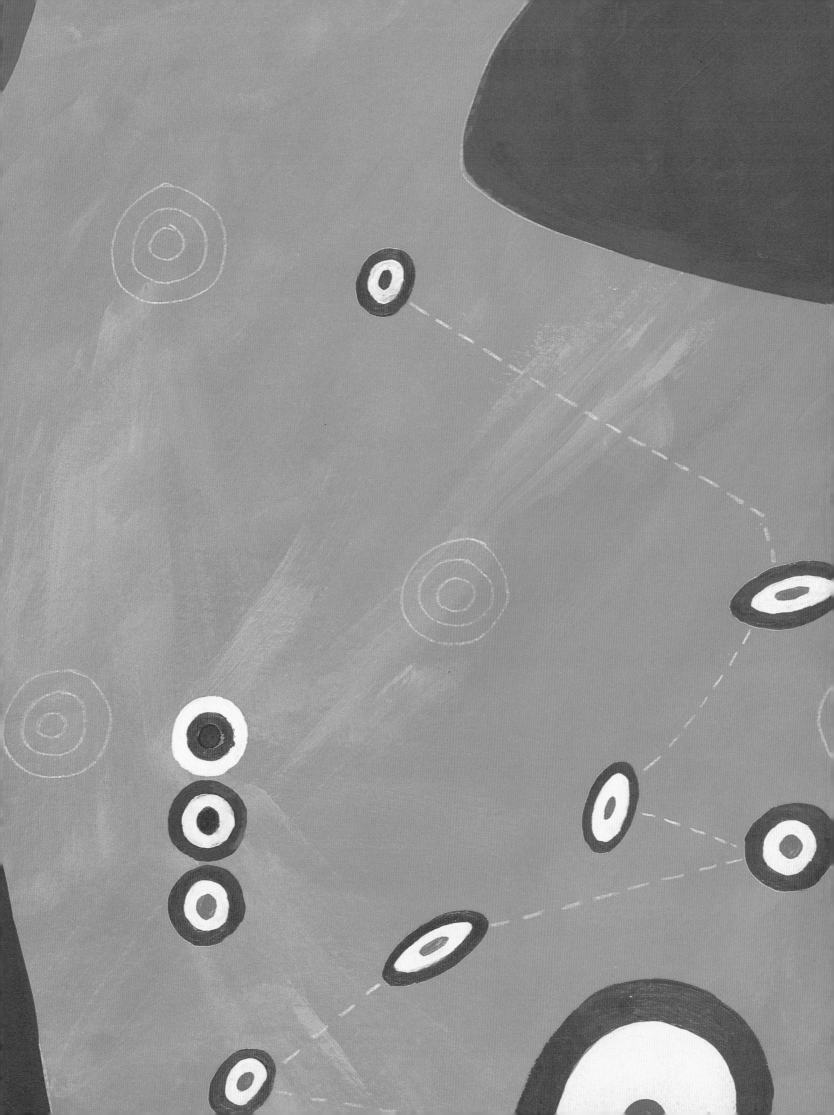